ETHAN'S FAVORITE TEACHER

Story by
Hila Colman

Pictures by
John Wallner

CROWN PUBLISHERS, INC., NEW YORK

Manufactured in the United States of America
Published simultaneously in Canada by General Publishing Company Limited
First Edition

The text of this book is set in 14 pt. Baskerville
The illustrations are pen and ink drawings reproduced in line with two
additional flat colors pre-separated by the artist.

Library of Congress Cataloging in Publication Data

Colman, Hila.
    Ethan's favorite teacher.

    SUMMARY: Bored at school, Ethan throws himself into
playing electronic tic-tac-toe games with an orangutan
at the zoo.
    [1. School stories] I. Wallner, John C., ill.
II. Title.
PZ7.C7Et   [E]   74-31081
ISBN 0-517-52114-8

For my favorite Ethan

"Get up, Ethan," his mother called, "or you'll be late
to school."

Ethan pulled the covers over his head. He didn't care if
he never went to school. Ethan hated school. To study was
boring. He especially hated doing the same thing over and
over again. If he didn't know the answer to an arithmetic
problem right away, he gave up.

But Ethan had to go to school. He got dressed, had his
breakfast, and managed to get to his classroom just as the
bell was ringing.

The first lesson had to be arithmetic!

"We'll do the multiplication tables," said Ethan's teacher. She pointed to Ethan. "How much is four times four?"

But Ethan wasn't listening. He was looking out of the window thinking of something else. Without realizing it, he muttered, "Why is the sky blue?"

The other children laughed, but his teacher got angry. "Pay attention," she scolded. "We are doing arithmetic now, not science. Betty, you give us the answer."

Betty was the smartest girl in the class. "Four times four is sixteen," she said promptly.

The teacher pointed to the other questions on the blackboard.

"Five times five is twenty-five," said another child.

"Six times six is thirty-six," shouted another.

But Ethan could not keep his mind on arithmetic. Out-
side the window he watched two birds chasing each other
across the sky.

"Ethan, stop daydreaming," scolded his teacher.

Ethan tried hard to think about the multiplication
tables, but his mind was filled with questions that no one
answered.

During recess, when he saw Betty he asked, "How many stars are there in the sky?"

"Count them yourself," she said. "You don't even know how much four times four is."

"And you don't know how many stars there are in the sky," he said.

At home, when Ethan was going to bed he asked, "Mom, why does it get dark at night?"

"You ask too many questions," she said. "It's time to turn out the light and go to sleep."

But Ethan lay in the dark wondering about all the things he wanted to know: What made thunder and lightning? Why was the grass green? It was a pain, he thought, to have to study dumb things like spelling and arithmetic instead of really important things.

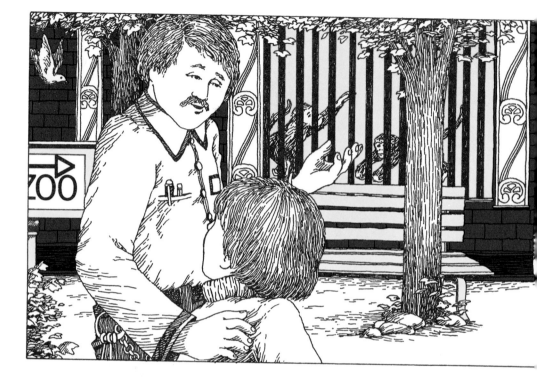

One place more important to Ethan than school was the zoo. It was near where he lived, and the next day Ethan went to the zoo after school. He loved to go there. He liked animals better than people. Except for Frank, the zoo keeper. Ethan followed Frank around from one cage to another and watched Frank throw food to the animals.

"Why do elephants have trunks?" asked Ethan.

"So that they can pick food up from the ground and also from high in the trees. That's how they eat," Frank told him.

"Why do zebras have stripes?" Ethan asked.

"Stripes are for their protection. When zebras roam the forest, the big animals can't see them so easily and go after them. The stripes are a camouflage."

"Why do some monkeys have tails and others don't?" Ethan asked.

"Because they're not all monkeys, that's why," Frank said. "Only monkeys have long tails. The others are apes. The orangutans, the chimpanzees, and that pair of big gorillas are all apes."

Ethan especially liked two orangutans, Sadie and Bill. He always stopped at their cage the longest.

One day he was surprised to find their cage empty.

"Where are Sadie and Bill?" he asked Frank.

"They're at school," Frank said.

"You're kidding," laughed Ethan. "Animals don't go to school."

"These two do. They're learning how to play tic-tac-toe."

Ethan laughed again. "That's a joke. Sadie and Bill can't read or write. How can they play tic-tac-toe?"

"You'll see. They're very smart and they study hard. They practice every day and that's what they're doing now. I bet they'll beat you."

"Not me. I'm smarter than any ape," Ethan said.

"Don't be so sure. Lots of animals can learn a lot of things. They learn by working hard and doing the same thing over and over again."

"That's boring," Ethan said.

A few weeks later Frank greeted Ethan with a big grin. "Do you want to play tic-tac-toe with Sadie?"

"Sure." Ethan was very excited. Frank took him to Sadie's cage. In front of the cage there was a big board with a tic-tac-toe game like this:

Frank explained to Ethan that the board was worked by an electronic device. "When Sadie pushes her button, a red light will flash in her box, and when you push yours, a yellow light will flash. You can go first," he said to Ethan.

Ethan pushed his button and sure enough a yellow light lit up his box. Then Sadie pushed her button. Her box flashed red. Ethan took another turn, and then Sadie. Then Ethan, then Sadie. Sadie won.

This time it was Sadie's turn to go first. Red, yellow, red, yellow, the lights flashed. Again Sadie won. But Ethan wouldn't give up. "Another game, another game," he kept calling. He played game after game with Sadie, and each time she won. Sadie jumped around her cage with delight. But Ethan got madder and madder.

"You'll see," he told Frank. "I'll beat her tomorrow."

"Maybe you will," Frank said. "Keep on trying."

Ethan went to the zoo every day that week to play tic-tac-toe with Sadie. She won every game. Ethan was very discouraged. If I can't beat an orangutan at tic-tac-toe, he thought, I must be dumb.

"It's not easy to beat her," Frank told him. "She works at it every day."

Ethan kept going over in his mind the games of tic-tac-toe he played with Sadie. If I had only made this move instead of that one, he thought, I could have beat her.

That evening, instead of watching TV, he sat at his desk and worked out tic-tac-toe games. He played one game after another, making believe that Sadie was his opponent.

For several nights he worked out tic-tac-toe games, until he was sure that he had figured out every possible move that Sadie could make.

"I never saw you work so hard," his mother said.

"This isn't work, it's fun," Ethan said.

His mother smiled. "That depends on how you look at it."

When Ethan went to the zoo to play with Sadie again, he was excited but a little nervous too. "She can go first," he said generously.

Sadie pushed her button and her box lit up red. Then Ethan pushed his yellow one. Then Sadie, then Ethan. On the seventh move, Sadie beat him.

"I give up," Ethan announced. "I'm not going to play with her anymore. I must be dumb."

"You're in too much of a hurry," Frank said. "Too impatient. Think, take your time before you make your move."

Frank persuaded him to play another game. Ethan went first this time. Then Sadie took her turn.

"You wait a minute," he said to Sadie. "I'm going to think." Sadie sat and scratched herself until he lit his square. Then Sadie flashed her box red.

Ethan stopped to think again before he made his next move.

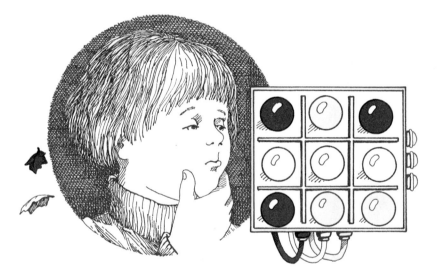

Sadie got very excited and pushed her button. A big grin lit up Ethan's face. The opening was there and he took it. ETHAN WON.

Sadie jumped around her cage wildly and beat her fists against the bars. Ethan laughed. "I won, I won," he cried.

Frank was pleased. "I'm glad to see someone give Sadie competition. She beats everyone who comes here."

Ethan felt very happy about beating Sadie. But in school Betty still made fun of him. "You're dumb! You're so dumb you think a seesaw is something to cut with," she said.

That got Ethan mad. "You're so dumb you can't spell with your eyes closed. Besides, I can be smart if I want." Betty laughed.

"Shut up," Ethan shouted.

One day the teacher said that she was going to take the class on a trip. "Where do you want to go?" she asked the children.

"Let's go to the zoo," said Ethan. "There's an orangutan who plays tic-tac-toe, and we can play with her."

The children laughed. "That's hard to believe," said the teacher.

"But it's true." Ethan was furious. "Call up the zoo and ask for Frank. He'll tell you. I've played with her."

The children laughed even harder. "Ethan plays with an ape, Ethan plays with an ape," they teased.

"She's smarter than any of you," Ethan yelled.

The next day the teacher said, "We owe Ethan an apology. There is an orangutan at the zoo who plays tic-tac-toe. We'll all go to see her in a few days."

Ethan could hardly wait. In the meantime he went to the zoo every afternoon after school to play the game with Sadie. He won some games and she won some games.

"I'd like to win every time," he told Frank.

"That wouldn't be any fun. She's smart and you're smart. That makes a better game. Besides, it doesn't matter who wins. You have a good time playing, don't you?"

"Yeah, sure. But I work hard at winning," said Ethan.

Frank laughed. "So does Sadie. But that's half the fun. If it was a snap you'd say it was boring. So would Sadie. That ape sure gets a kick out of learning."

Ethan worried about what was going to happen when he went to the zoo with his class.

When the day finally arrived, the class lined up two by two, and their teacher walked them over to the zoo. As they went from cage to cage, Ethan told the children why the elephants had trunks and why the zebras had stripes. He explained to them which were monkeys and which were apes. His teacher looked surprised.

But it was the orangutan's cage that Ethan was waiting for. He wanted the class to see his friend Sadie. Sadie jumped up and down when Ethan walked up to her cage. "Betty, you play with Sadie first," Ethan cried.

"Sure. I can beat a dumb ape," Betty said.

The children gathered around while Sadie and Betty played tic-tac-toe. Sadie pressed her button, and Betty pressed hers. One box after another lit up: red, yellow, red, yellow. Sadie won.

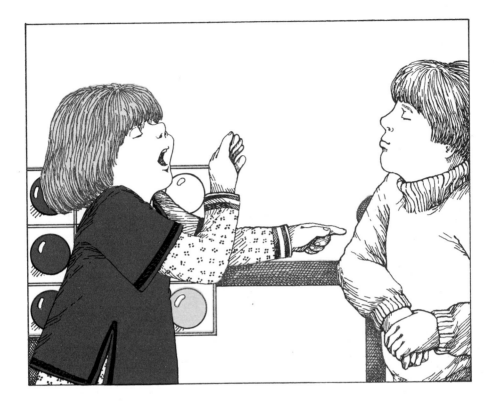

"That was just for practice," Betty said. "I'll beat her next time."

Again the boxes flashed: yellow, red, yellow, red.

Again Betty lost. They played five games and Betty lost every one.

"None of us can beat her if Betty can't," the children said. "Betty's the smartest one in the class."

"Let me try," Ethan said.

Betty laughed. "If I can't beat her, neither can you, dumb-dumb."

"We don't have much time," the teacher said, "but let
Ethan have a chance."

Ethan walked up close to the cage and looked right into
Sadie's eyes. He thought she smiled at him.

Ethan let Sadie make the first move. She lit a corner box
red. He lit the center box yellow. She lit another corner
red, and he put his yellow in between her two red. One
after another they played, and neither one of them won.

"See, you can't beat her," laughed Betty.

"But she didn't beat me either," said Ethan. "Can I play
one more game?" he asked the teacher.

"Just one more and then we have to go," she said.

Ethan didn't think about Betty, he didn't think about the children watching him. All he thought about was the tic-tac-toe board, and every move he had to make. He made his first move. Sadie made her move. Then Ethan. Then Sadie made a mistake. Ethan won!

All the children clapped. All except for Betty. "It was just luck," said she.

"No, it wasn't," argued Ethan. "I figured it out. I can beat her a lot."

"She still beats you too," Betty said.

"Who cares?" said Ethan.

"You must have worked hard," his teacher said.

Ethan shook his head. "It was fun."

His teacher laughed. "Sadie's a good teacher. You never study in school. Maybe you will now."

Ethan laughed too. It was pretty funny to think of an ape who couldn't read or write as a teacher. Ethan waved good-bye to Sadie. "I guess she's a pretty smart ape," he said, and he went back to school with his class.